A Happy Day for Ramona

A Happy Day for Ramona

and Other Missionary Stories for Children

Compiled from past issues of *The Alliance World* (a missionary education tool published by Christian Publications)

Illustrated by Janis Treat Timyan

CHRISTIAN PUBLICATIONS / Camp Hill, Pennsylvania

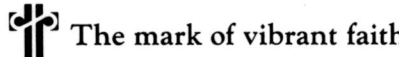 The mark of vibrant faith

Christian Publications
Publishing House of The Christian and Missionary Alliance
3825 Hartzdale Drive, Camp Hill, PA 17011

© 1987 by Christian Publications. All rights reserved
ISBN: 0-87509-392-2 LOC Catalog Card Number: 87-71018
Printed in the United States of America

All stories written by Velma B. Kiefer for *The Alliance World* from material supplied by Alliance missionaries.

Scripture quotations are from the HOLY BIBLE: NEW INTERNATIONAL VERSION. Copyright © 1973, 1978, 1984 by the International Bible Society. Used by permission of Zondervan Bible Publishers.

Contents

A Happy Day for Ramona   1
(Submitted by Kay Esparza—Mexico)

An MK in Korea   7
(Submitted by Cindi Strong—Korea)

A Singing Missionary   13
(Submitted by Carolyn Welty—Ecuador)

Sampat's Treasure   19
(Submitted by Winifred Sanford—India)

Happy Rollers   27
(Submitted by Jane Landaow—Japan)

A New Mother   33
(Submitted by The Christian and Missionary Alliance in Canada)

Naomi's Promise   39
(Submitted by Naomi Ord—Colombia)

Kill the Missionaries!   45
(Submitted by Shirley Maxey—Irian Jaya)

She Heard It on the Radio   53
(Submitted by Rev. Donald Weidemann—Hong Kong)

A Happy Day for Ramona

It was Monday morning in Saltillo, Mexico, and eight-year-old Ramona was excited. She was going to attend a new kind of school on this day. She could hardly wait to see what it would be like. But before she could go, she had to do her morning chores. And she would have to hurry. Ramona jumped out of bed and pulled on her clothes. She dashed out of the bedroom and ran across the courtyard into the kitchen.

Her mother was already busy preparing breakfast.

"Buenos dias, Mamacita," (Good morning, Mother) called Ramona cheerfully. "Is the corn ready to be ground?"

"Yes," nodded Mother, "here it is." She set a pail of steaming corn on the floor near Ramona. "But be careful now. It is *very* hot."

Ramona picked the pail up carefully. Down the street she hurried to the tortilleria. The tortilleria was the place where families went to have their corn ground into *masa* or corn dough.

By the time she reached it, there was already a long line of children and mothers ahead of her. Ramona got in line to wait her turn. It seemed as if her turn would never come this morning. But at last it did, and the corn was ground into *masa*.

Ramona lugged the pail of heavy wet corn dough back home. And she and her mother began to make tortillas. For each tortilla they pinched off a small ball of *masa*. Gently they patted the dough back and forth in their hands to form it into a round bread that looked like a thin pancake. They laid each piece on a hot griddle. The toasty corn smell of the tortillas on the griddle made Ramona hungry.

Then Mother used the tortillas to make delicious sandwiches filled with refried beans. We call them tacos. And she poured cups of steaming *caleche* (kah-le-che), boiled milk with a bit of instant coffee and sugar.

Ramona smiled, "Que sabroso." (This is yummy.)

But when breakfast was over Ramona had still more chores to do before she could go to the special school.

Ramona lived in an adobe (mud) brick house. The rooms of her home were built around a pretty courtyard. And one of her jobs was to sweep and wash the floor of the courtyard each morning. Another was to water the flowers. Clay pots filled with geraniums hung around the courtyard walls.

Ramona liked their big, bright red flowers. But this morning she wished there were not so many of them to water. She scurried from one to the other, spilling some water on the floor.

Finally, her chores were finished. Ramona ran to get ready for school. Quickly she combed her long, shiny black hair and smoothed her dress. Her big dark eyes glowed with excitement as she ran to kiss her mother goodbye.

It was almost 8:30 in the morning. She did not want to be late to school on the very first day. Ramona hurried out of the house and started walking up the hill.

Today she had no time to notice the grand mountains all around Saltillo. She did not even glance at the nice old houses along the way. There was no time to wander off and watch the weavers weaving beautiful woolen blankets or to stop and see the silversmiths making fine silver pieces.

As Ramona hurried up the steep hills, she wondered what would happen at the special school. You see, Ramona had been invited to Vacation Bible School. She wondered, *What will it be like? What will we do there?*

She did not have to wait long to find out. She arrived at the church just in time to join her friend Llanet and march into the building.

All morning Ramona was busy singing, listening, learning, playing and doing handwork. Vacation Bible School seemed to be the nicest kind of school. Ramona was glad that she had come. She could not wait to get home to tell her mother all about it.

She almost ran down the steep hills to her home. When she got there she rushed into the kitchen to find her mother. The kitchen was filled with the aroma of red chili peppers. Ramona loved that smell. It must mean *enchiladas* for lunch. Mm-m-m! As Ramona ate her lunch she bubbled over with talk about the school. In her excitement she ate as fast as she talked.

After lunch, when the dishes were washed, Ramona and her mother sat in the *sala* or living room. It was time for a crocheting lesson. Carefully Ramona hooked the needle around the thread and pulled it through loop stitches.

She counted the stitches just as her mother had taught her. But all during the crocheting time, Ramona was still talking about Vacation Bible School. She told her mother all about the songs, the Bible story, the handwork and the games. She was looking forward to tomorrow.

The next day, after her chores, Ramona was allowed to go to school again. And she liked the second day just as well as the first.

That morning the pastor, Pastor Reyes, announced, "We are also having special meetings here at the church each evening. We invite you all to come and to bring your parents with you."

Ramona was delighted. She decided, *As soon as school is over I'll go straight home and invite my whole family to come.* And that is what she did. But her mother and father were not as happy and excited about the invitation as she was. They did not seem interested in going to church. Ramona begged and coaxed everyone to go. At last, to end the coaxing, mother, father, her big sister—and two cousins—agreed. "All right, we'll go this one time." And they all went with her.

How pleased Ramona was to march off up the hills and into the church with her whole family! But before the evening was over she was even happier.

The speaker, Rev. Esparza, spoke about a loving Savior and what He has done for us. And afterward, he invited everyone who wanted to belong to the Lord Jesus to come to the front of the church. A wonderful thing then happened. Ramona—and her whole family—stood up. They stepped into the aisle and walked to the front of the church. All of them wanted to trust in Jesus as their Savior. What a happy day for Ramona!

An MK in Korea

Suppose *your* dad and mom said, "We think God wants us to be missionaries. We believe He wants us to go to another country to serve Him."

What would you say? How would you like to move to a strange place far from home? How would you feel about leaving your friends, your school and the things you like?

A young boy named Joshua knows how it feels. That is what happened to him. Why don't we hear what he said about being an MK—a missionary kid.

My dad and mom felt that God wanted them to be missionaries. They believed it was His good plan for our family. We talked a lot about it. We talked about how important it is to obey God and go tell others about Jesus. And we read missionary stories.

But most of all we prayed. We prayed that God would show us where He wanted us to serve Him. And we asked Him what He wanted us to do. He answered our prayers by showing Mom and Dad that He wanted our family to go to Korea. And we began to get ready. By then I was eight years old.

Soon it was time to leave our town—and country—and I felt sad. I felt sad about leaving my best friends, my dog and my bike. I knew I would miss them.

I didn't cry as I said goodbye. God helped me to leave my grandma and grandpa and my friends and things. I only cried as our plane started to land in Seoul, Korea. Everything looked so strange and different. Besides, I was tired from the long trip.

But now I am 9 years old—almost 10. And I am finding out that being an MK in Korea is special.

I live in a nice house across from Seoul Foreign School. It's a Christian school. We have math and the other classes you have. And we have Bible study and memory work, too.

In some ways Korea is like the United States. You can buy ice cream cones and donuts. You can play baseball and even video games.

But some things are different. The language is very different. At first it sounded so strange, but my ears are used to it now. I can even understand and speak a few Korean words.

You know, we take off our shoes before going into a house. And in Korean homes and in some churches we sit on cushions on the floor instead of chairs. Instead of sleeping in beds, we sleep on mats on the floor. The floors are warm. They are heated by warm air pipes under the floor. On a cold winter day it feels nice to sit or sleep on a warm floor.

For snacks we may eat sweet apples, big pears or juicy tangerines. Or we nibble toasted barley puffs, puffed rice, dried cuttlefish or fish chips.

Sometimes we visit Korean families, and they serve us a big Korean meal. They serve things like rice, fish, vegetables and peppery, pickled cabbage. Some of their foods look and taste strange to me. But I try to be polite and eat them. Most people think Korean meals are delicious. I'll probably learn to eat the new foods and think they taste great, too.

Seoul, the city in which we live, is a really big city. It has 9 million people! And it is the capital of South Korea.

No matter which direction you look, you see churches. They are easy to see, because they have crosses on the steeples. That makes it simple to find them.

Every Sunday my family and I ride to church—not in a family car, but in a taxi. The church we go to is big. More than 2,000 people belong to it. And you should hear them sing and pray. The Korean Christians are full of love for the Lord. Gladly they gather to praise and worship Him.

Sunday school is not in the morning but in the afternoon, and they have some big Sunday schools.

You probably wonder why, if there are

so many churches, we need to be here. Well, there are many, many people who are not Christians, who do not go to church. And Mom says that there are still 1,000 villages that do not have any churches at all.

Mostly I like Korea. Sometimes in winter I get cold waiting for buses or taxis. Now and then we get caught downtown during an air raid practice. Then we have to wait until a siren blows "all clear" before we can go on our way again. There are even practice air raids at night. That is a little scary. All of a sudden the sirens blow loudly, lights are turned off and jet planes roar into the sky. I am always glad when the pretend raids are over.

The Koreans are very friendly. They love fun and jokes and like to celebrate holidays. They celebrate New Year's Day, Independence Day, Children's Day, Moon Festival Day (a thanksgiving day), Christmas, Alphabet Day and other holidays. They celebrate with contests, games, parades, sports and food.

You should see some of the contests. There are wrestling and kite-flying contests for boys. Girls have seesaw contests. They balance their seesaw boards on a roll of straw. The girls stand on the ends of the board. They take turns jumping down hard on the end to bounce each other into the air.

Girls also have swinging contests. They hang long swings from high trees. Then the girls stand up on the swings and pump as hard as they can. They swing far back and high up into the air. People come to see who can swing the highest—who will be the winner.

Well, that is about all I can think of to tell you now. I keep seeing and learning new things all the time. The longer we are in Korea, the more I like it.

I'm glad our family came here. Will you pray for missionary kids and their parents? Pray that we may help tell the friendly Koreans about their best and greatest Friend—and Savior—Jesus.

A Singing Missionary

Can anyone be a missionary? No? Who may be a missionary? How old must you be to serve the Lord as a missionary? Are six-, seven- and eight-year-old boys and girls old enough?

When Michael was only two years old, he once served the Lord as a missionary in Ecuador. How could such a little boy do anything? What did he do? His mother tells us the story.

Every Thursday, Michael (Miguelito in Spanish) and I drove to a certain mountain. We parked our car at the bottom of the mountain and hiked up a zigzag trail. We hiked to a church in the village of Peguche.

On our way we had to walk over a footbridge that crossed a tumbling stream. I did not like to cross that bridge at all. It frightened me because there were holes in it. Through the holes I could see the rushing stream below us. I held Miguelito's hand tightly in mine and stepped carefully.

After crossing the bridge, we followed the trail until we reached the village. Huffing and puffing, we arrived at the little church in Peguche.

We had already visited all the families in this village. But when we told them we had come to talk with them about Jesus, guess what happened. Many people slammed their doors in our faces. They did not want to hear about Jesus. They would not listen to us. That was discouraging.

Yet I had a ladies' class every week at the church. While I sat in the class, Miguelito usually played out-of-doors. He and an older girl played in a pile of dirt in front of the church. Now and then I glanced out to see that he was all right. But once when I looked, I did not see Miguelito. He was gone. He had tired of playing in the dirt. He had wandered away to find something else to do.

The ladies and I jumped up. We all ran outside to look for him. "Where's Miguelito?" I asked the girl who had been playing with him.

"I don't know," she answered. "He went that way." She pointed down the trail toward the dangerous bridge. My heart pounded. Down the mountain I rushed toward the bridge.

"Miguelito, Miguelito," I called, as I ran up to the bridge. I was afraid to look down at the rushing water. But I did. There was no sign of Miguelito anywhere. I was frightened and worried. Where could he be?

I scrambled back up the path calling

his name over and over. Miguelito did not answer my calls. Then I saw a woman beckoning to me. I stopped. "Have you seen my son?"

"Yes," she nodded and pointed to a house farther up the trail. "He went into that house."

I ran to the house and hurried around it to the courtyard in the back. Then I stood still and stared. How relieved I was! There sat Miguelito, cross-legged on the dirt floor, with a circle of children. They were eating mote (hominy) and tostado (parched corn)—and singing!

Miguelito was teaching the boys and girls a Quechua Jesus-song that he had learned in Sunday school. The children were trying their best to sing it with him. My fear turned to joy. I smiled a big wide smile. "Thank you, Lord."

I explained to the mother in that home what had happened. She nodded her head understandingly. I could see that she was delighted to have Miguelito visit and sing with her children. Afterward, when we had said goodbye and were ready to leave, the mother smiled at Miguelito, "Come back again—anytime."

"Thank you, Lord," I whispered to myself.

This same mother had slammed her door in our faces when we had tried to visit her before. She would not listen to us or talk with us.

I knew that the Lord had caused Miguelito to wander over to her home for a visit. The Lord had put it in his heart to sing Jesus-songs and to teach the children to sing them with him. The Lord had opened the family's hearts through Miguelito's friendly visit.

But that was not all the Lord did. He gave that family willingness to hear about the Savior. The children started going to Sunday school in the village church. After a while, the parents wandered into the little church, too. Then some aunts, uncles and cousins began to come to services. And something wonderful happened. Within a year many of the children and grown-ups in that big family had accepted the Lord as their Savior. And that all happened because of my friendly little Miguelito—a two-year-old singing missionary. Again I say, "Thank you, Lord."

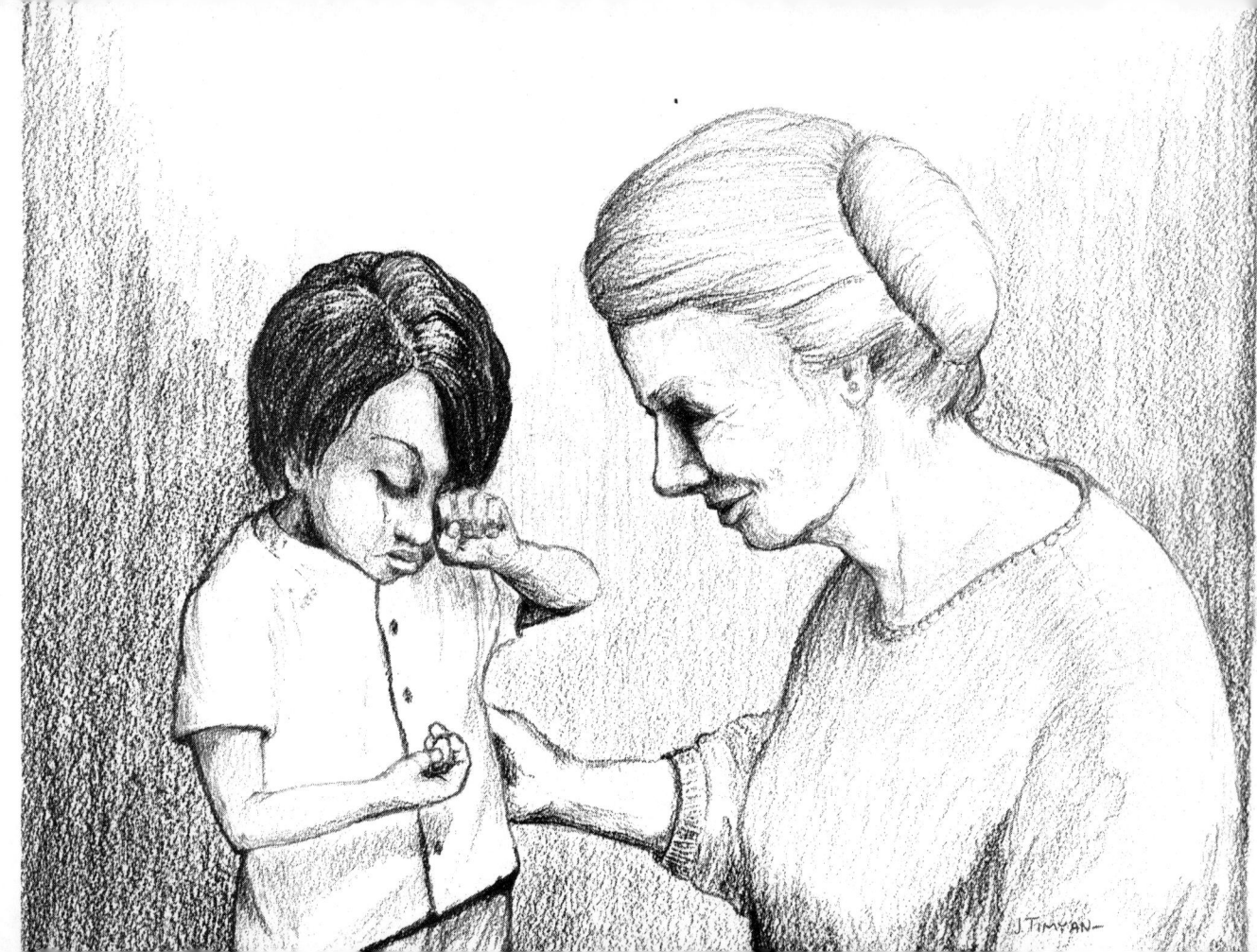

Sampat's Treasure

Do you have some favorite thing that you like more than anything else? Something that you would never want to lose or give away? What is it? Is it a beautiful seashell, a special stone or a toy or a pet?

Sampat, a little boy in India, had a favorite thing—a treasure. It was so precious to him that he took it with him everywhere he went—even to bed. I am sure you can't guess what it was. So I'll tell you in this story.

Sampat lived at the Mission Boys' School at Akola. But he could not go to school. He was only three years old. So he just followed Auntie, the missionary, wherever she went. One day Auntie said to Sampat, "How would you like to learn a song in English?" Sampat beamed. And Auntie taught him to sing a stanza and the chorus of "Joy Bells in My Heart."

Sampat could hardly wait to sing the new song for the older boys. How proud they were of him! He was like a little brother to all of them. Afterward, whenever a visitor came to the school, someone would always ask, "Sampat, will you sing 'Joy Bells' for the visitor?" And Sampat was delighted to sing his song.

Eventually, the mission leader heard about Sampat's song. One day when he visited the school he said, "Sampat, if you will sing 'Joy Bells' for me I will give you a pice (rhymes with ice and is worth 1/4 penny)." To Sampat that was a lot of money.

He stood up straight and sang in his best voice. The man thanked him and dropped a pice into his hand. Never had Sampat been so excited. To him the pice seemed like a million dollars. He clasped it tight in his fist, and from that day on, Sampat carried the precious penny with him wherever he went—even to bed. Often, while he slept, the penny slipped out of his hand. Then he would waken the boys near him to look for it. You can imagine how the boys liked that!

Sampat was happy at the mission school, but there was a problem. There were too many boys. Already there were more than 100. And more new boys kept coming to live at the school. There was not enough space on the floor for everyone to sleep. It was getting too crowded.

Auntie made room for some boys to sleep in her house. They slept on the living room floor, the dining room floor and even under her bed. But still more boys came.

Auntie was concerned. "Something must be done," she said. Suddenly she had an idea. "I'll invite the men of the building committee to come to school. Then I'll ring the go-to-bed bell. All the boys will go to bed on the floor just as they do at night. When the men see how the boys must squeeze together to sleep, they will help us."

That was what Auntie did. And she was right.

When the men looked into the crowded boys' house, they shook their heads. Then they looked into Auntie's house. There were boys everywhere—floors covered with them. The men agreed with Auntie, "Something must be done."

They said, "Look, we'll give your house to the boys' school. They can use all of its rooms. And we'll build you a new little house on the hill across the street."

The men hurried to the other side of the street. They marched around and measured how big Auntie's house should be. When they finished they said, "You really do need another building, and we would like to build you one . . . but . . . we have no money to pay for it."

After the men had gone, the boys asked, "Auntie, why did those men measure the ground across the street?" She explained, "Well, they would like to build a new house for me. Then more boys could move into my old house and sleep there. But, there isn't enough money for a new house."

"Can't God give us money?" asked the boys. "Yes, He can," nodded Auntie, "and we'll pray hard that He will."

So the boys began to pray. Three times a day, before each meal, they prayed, "Lord, send us a house for Auntie." They were sure that God would answer their prayer—so sure that they would go outside and look across the street to see if God had sent the house and put it on the hill. Three weeks long they prayed.

Then one evening at prayer time Auntie talked with them about the Bible verse which says, "Whatever He (Jesus) says to you, do it. If Jesus asks you to give Him your heart, do it," said Auntie. "If He asks you to give Him your life, do it. If one day you have some money, and He asks you for it, give it to Him. Obey Jesus. Do what He says."

The next day one of the boys called, "Auntie, come quick, Sampat is sick." But before Auntie could go to see Sampat, he came to her. He was crying loudly and holding his precious pice tightly in his fist. He looked up at Auntie and held out his hand. "Here," he sobbed. "Here, take my pice and build your house."

Auntie did not take the penny. She did not understand. "Here," repeated Sampat, "take my pice and build your house."

"Sampat, what are you talking about?" asked Auntie.

"Didn't you tell us last night that we should do whatever Jesus told us to do?" asked Sampat.

"Yes, I told you that."

"Well, Jesus told me to give you my pice to build your house. I don't want to give it, but here, take it."

Auntie did not want to take Sampat's penny. But she had to. The Lord had told him to give it to her.

Still crying, Sampat turned and walked away. And Auntie hurried into her house. She sat down and wrote a letter to her sister about Sampat's pice—how he gave his precious penny to her because Jesus told him to.

When Auntie's sister read the letter about Sampat's pice, she gave it to friends to read. The church friends who read about Sampat's gift were delighted. They sat right down and wrote a surprise letter to Auntie. They wrote, "If you will send us Sampat's precious pice, we will send you $4,000 to build your house."

Auntie laughed for joy and praised the Lord. Quickly she wrapped up Sampat's pice and mailed it to the United States. Back came a check for $4,000. Up went a new little house for Auntie. Into Auntie's old house moved some happy boys. Everyone thanked the Lord for the wonderful answer to their prayers.

Joy bells rang in little Sampat's heart. He believed that his precious penny paid for Auntie's house. And it did. Because he gave his pice, friends in America sent $4,000 to build the house. How happy Sampat was that he had done what Jesus told him to do!

You will be happy, too, if you obey the Lord Jesus. God promised, "Blessed [happy] are all who fear the Lord, who walk in His ways" (Psalm 128:1).

Happy Rollers

Five-year-old Jill laughed with delight. What made her so happy? An older American friend had just handed her a gift—a pair of used roller skates. Jill lives in Japan with her missionary parents, and she was not able to bring any roller skates when she moved.

"These skates are too small for me now," explained Jill's friend, "I thought they might fit you."

Jill nearly jumped up and down with excitement. Roller skates! What fun! She couldn't wait to try them out. She thought that all she needed to do was put them on, stand up and start skating.

Jill's mother had other thoughts. "Oh, dear! I can just see all the skinned knees Jill is going to have—the bumps and bruises. How many falls she'll take! And how many tears she'll shed!"

Quickly Jill sat down with her friend to check the size of the roller skates. But what a disappointment! The skates were at least two sizes too big! Jill's face fell. She would have to wait awhile before she could go rolling merrily around the neighborhood.

Mother and Jill looked for a good place to keep the skates until later. They decided to put them into the shoe closet until Jill's feet grew a few sizes larger. There the skates sat and waited. It looked as if they would be resting quietly for a long time.

But one day something happened. Two eight-year-old neighbor girls, Naoka and Rie, came to play with Jill. Mother and Jill had invited the two girls to Sunday school, but they had never come.

Mother wondered, *How can we get Naoka and Rie interested in coming to the Sunday school in our house? What can we do that will make them want to come?*

Then the girls happened to see Jill's roller skates sitting in the shoe closet. They looked at the skates longingly, wishing to try them out. But they were much too polite to ask.

Mother saw the wish in the girls' eyes and faces. She smiled, stooped and picked up the skates. "Naoka and Rie, I think these skates might be just your size. Would you like to learn to roller skate?"

The girls nodded eagerly. "We'd love to."

Mother helped Naoka to put the skates on and stand up. Naoka wobbled uncertainly. How strange it felt to stand up on four little wheels. She leaned forward. Oops! She leaned backward. Suddenly her feet rolled away from her and—crash—she sat down hard. Naoka looked surprised and laughed. She picked herself up and tried again.

Slowly she put one foot forward. The skate rolled a few inches. She giggled. Carefully she moved the other foot. What fun! In just a little while, after a few more falls, Naoka skated slowly down the street to her home—and back. Jill jumped up and down, "Look at Naoka! Look! She can do it."

Then it was Rie's turn to try. She was a wee bit afraid. But she put on the skates and stood up. She wobbled and waved her arms trying to keep her balance. She grabbed Naoka and held onto her to keep from falling. Soon she let go of Naoka and tried to make the skates roll.

Several times she fell on her knees and sat down hard on the street. But Rie did not give up. Each time she picked herself up, brushed herself off and tried again. And after a while she could skate slowly. "Look at me. See! Watch what I can do."

Jill and her mother were happy for Rie and Naoka. But Jill sighed, "I want to skate, too. How long will it be before I'm big enough?"

Then it was time for Naoka and Rie to go home. But they came back the next day and the next. In a few days they were skating up and down the street, giggling happily.

And then something nice happened. Both girls started coming to the Sunday school at Jill's house. They began to hear the wonderful stories of Jesus and His love. They learned to sing songs about Him, and they memorized Bible verses. Now they were glad to come to Sunday school. They liked it so much that on rainy days they even came to Jill's house to play Sunday school with her.

But that is not the end of the story. Two other neighbor sisters, Yumiko and Yoho, had been watching the happy roller skaters on the street. Secretly, they wished that they could put on the skates and have a turn learning to roll on the little wheels. It looked like such fun.

Happily Jill shared her gift skates with Yumiko and Yoho, too. Now they are learning to skate without falling down or crashing into things. And guess what? They have started coming to Sunday school, too.

Mother and Jill are delighted that two more neighbors are coming to hear God's Word. And they thank the Lord. He is the One who caused Jill's friend to give her skates to Jill. He helped Jill to share the too-big skates. He used the skates to make friends with *four* neighbors and to interest them in coming to Sunday school.

Jill and her mother wonder, *How many more neighbors will want to learn to roller skate—and come to Sunday school?*

Jill's mother prays that the four neighbor girls will soon understand that Jesus has a gift for them—a gift which will give them much greater joy than roller skating.

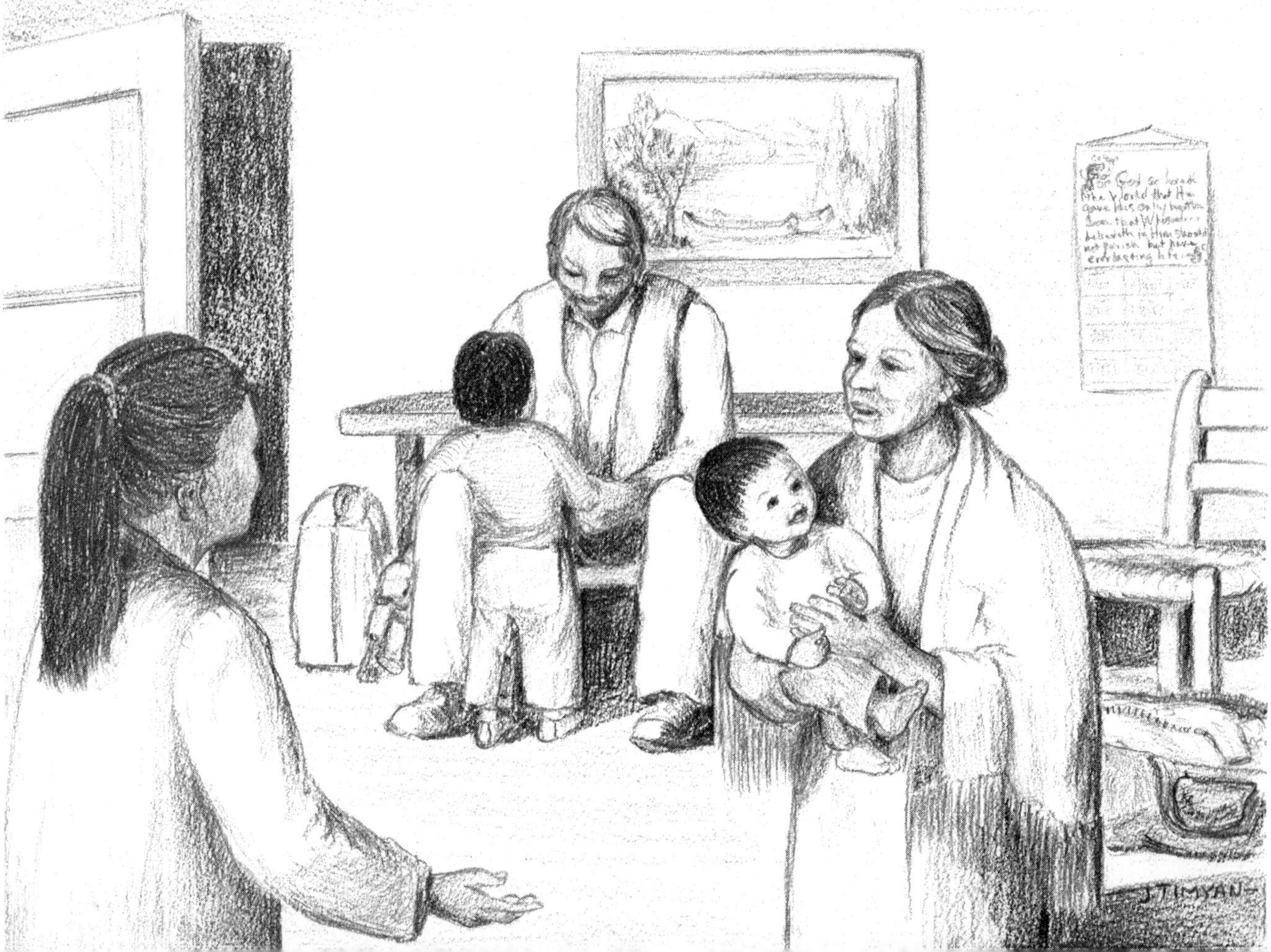
J. TIMYAN

A New Mother

What do you mean when you say that someone is selfish? What is selfishness? A selfish boy thinks only about himself and what he likes. He takes the biggest piece of cake, pushes to be first in line, wants the first turn and sits in the best seat. Are children the only ones who are selfish? In what ways are some grown-ups selfish?

Would it make you happy to be selfish? No! Selfishness can only bring unhappiness to you and to others. A Cree Indian mother found that out.

This young Indian mother lived in Saint Boniface, Manitoba. She had two pretty babies with shiny black hair, a chubby boy named Richard and a plump baby girl named Delores.

Taking care of babies is a lot of work. Babies must be bathed, dressed and fed. They wear diapers that have to be changed, and their clothes must be washed. During the day they must be put to bed for naps and comforted when they cry. This selfish mother did not like having to stay home all day to take care of her two babies. She got tired of it. She wanted to go places and have fun doing whatever *she* liked to do.

At last one day the mother decided

that she had had enough. She packed up and left her husband and children. Off she hurried to do as she pleased. She thought that would make her happy.

What about little Richard and Delores? They were upset and cried. They did not understand what was happening. Where was their mother? Why didn't she come home?

Grandma and Grandpa took the children to live at their house. They hugged and loved their grandchildren and took good care of them. Richard and Delores missed their mother, but they soon felt at home with Grandma and Grandpa.

One day there was a knock on Grandma's door. When she opened the door, guess who stood there: Richard and Delores's mother! She had come to visit them! But it was not a happy visit because she was still thinking only about herself. She did not really care much about anyone else. Soon she said goodbye to the children and went away again. Richard and Delores felt sad. *Why doesn't Mama stay with us?* they wondered.

Every once in a while the mother came to visit Grandma, Grandpa and the children. But it was always the same: hi and goodbye!

In a few years Richard and Delores were old enough to go to school. The first year they attended school in the town where Grandma and Grandpa lived. But the second year they went away to another school—a boarding school. They lived at the school during the week and spent the weekend with their grandparents.

Now and then their mother dropped by for the weekend. But she was usually restless and unhappy. Richard always hoped that she would play and talk with them, but she didn't. Instead she would go away for hours, and come back late at night when the children were asleep.

Then something happened—and suddenly everything was different. One weekend when their mother came for a visit, Richard and Delores could not believe their eyes. They stood and stared at her. She did not look the same at all. Instead of being sad, she looked glad. Her eyes were bright and shining as if a light had been turned on inside her. She walked with happy, bouncy steps. She played with Richard and Delores and even hugged and kissed them. They were really puzzled. What had happened to their mother? What did it mean?

Then their mother called them to her. She said, "I have something to tell you—something wonderful." The children's eyes opened wide. What did their mother have to tell them? Would she tell them a secret—the secret of her being different?

Quietly, then, mother told them that

she had heard some good news—the Good News about God's Son, Jesus. She had trusted Him to be her Savior from sin and sadness. The Lord had forgiven all her selfishness and all her other sin, too. He had put His love into her heart. He had made her His child, and one day He was going to take her to be where He is—to heaven.

Richard and Delores nearly jumped up and down for joy. Jesus, about whom they had heard at Christmas and Easter, was real! He had given them a new Mama—He had changed her from a selfish mother into a loving, happy one. If Jesus loved Mama so much, did He love them, too?

Their mother hugged them and told them of Christ's great love. After Richard and Delores heard what our loving Savior had done for them, they thanked Him and asked Him to live in their hearts, too. What a joyful evening that was!

How excited Richard and Delores were when they went back to school on Monday. But they would have been still more excited if they had known what the Lord was going to do next. He had something else in mind for them. I wonder if you could guess what it was?

The Lord was going to make them into a loving Christian family. He sent a Christian man into their lives, a man who loved Mama and Richard and Delores. Their mother and this man were married. And in June, as soon as school ended, Richard and his sister moved. They moved from Grandma and Grandpa's house to their new home with Mother—and Dad. Richard and Delores were delighted to live with a mother and father just like their friends did.

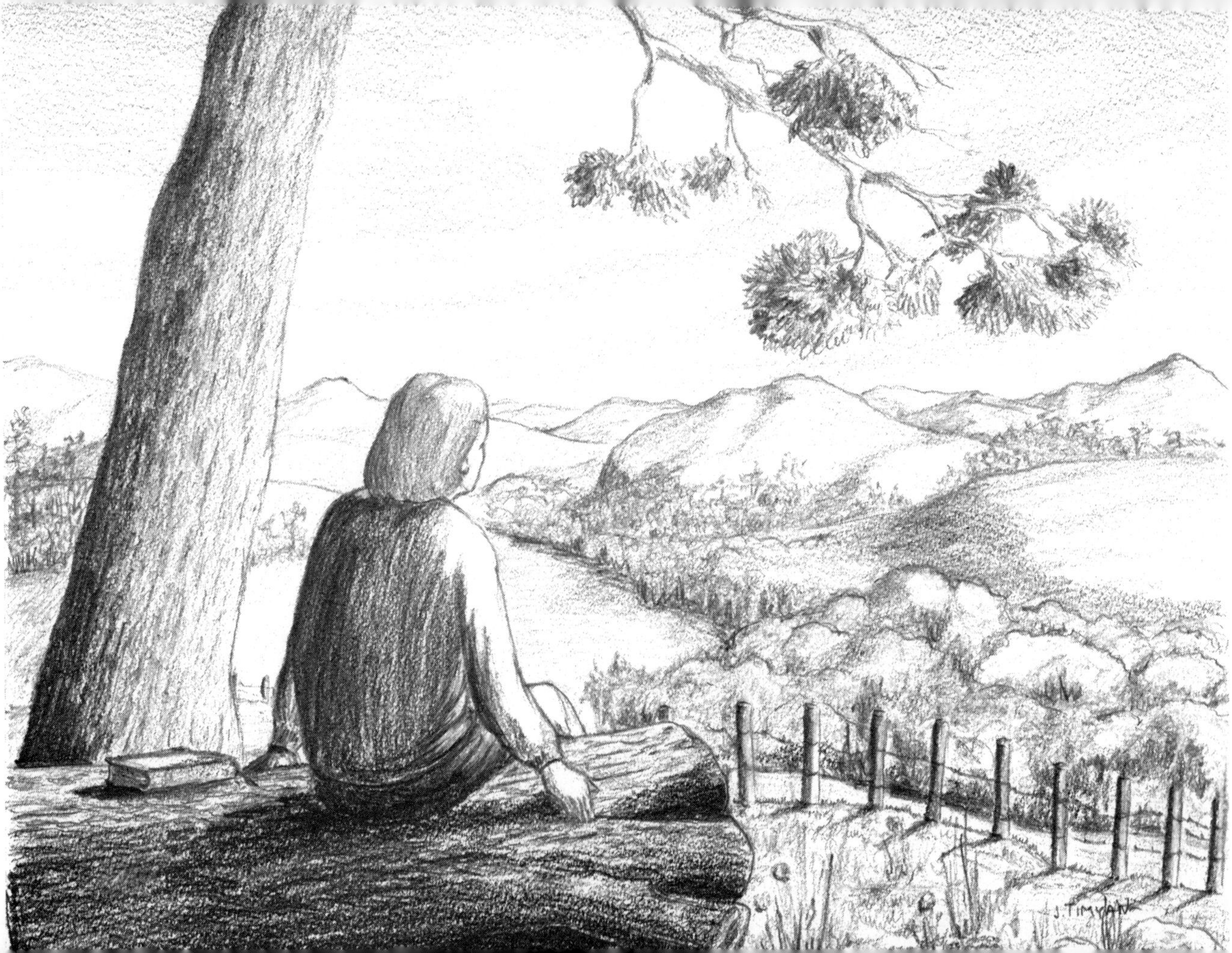
J. TIMYAN

Naomi's Promise

Why should you be careful about making promises? Why is it important to keep the promises that you make? What if you change your mind after you make a promise?

A few years ago a teenager named Naomi made God a promise and then . . . let me tell you why she made a promise and what happened.

Naomi was excited, happy and wide awake even though it was two o'clock in the morning. She sat in a large plane at Miami airport. Down the runway the plane roared. Up into the sky it climbed and headed south over the ocean.

Naomi was on her way to Camp Ebenezer in Colombia, South America. She could not wait to get to camp. Children and young people from all over Colombia would be there.

For two weeks Naomi was going to serve as a missionary helper. As the plane roared through the night sky, she dreamed. She dreamed about helping children and young people have fun at Camp Ebenezer. But most of all she dreamed about helping them to know and love the Lord Jesus. Naomi's eyes were shining with joy. She prayed, "Lord, use me."

It did not seem long before the plane was gliding down for a landing on the Colombian airfield. Soon the big plane had rolled to a stop, and Naomi walked down the ramp. Smiling missionary friends greeted and welcomed her to Colombia. And in a little while she was on her way to Camp Ebenezer.

Quickly Naomi explored the campground. She looked into the tabernacle and the rooms where they would be sleeping. She strolled out on the hill in back of the tabernacle. What a nice place for a camp!

Then Naomi met the campers. She loved the children and young people with their flashing dark eyes and shy, friendly smiles. *How pretty they are,* thought Naomi. *But how am I ever going to remember all their names?*

Camp began, and it was just great. There was lots of singing, fun, games, devotions, prayer and most important, Bible study. But there was one problem. And it was a *big* problem. Naomi became more and more upset about it. At last one morning she sat down on the hill in back of the tabernacle and cried. What was wrong? Why was Naomi crying?

The problem was that the campers spoke Spanish and Naomi spoke only English. More than anything she wanted to talk with the children and young people about the Savior. But she couldn't. Tears streamed down Naomi's cheeks.

A missionary friend named Kathy laid her hand on Naomi's shoulder. She said quietly, "Love does not need words. It can be communicated without them." Naomi stopped crying. Kathy was right. She could show Jesus' love by being joyful, helpful, kind and encouraging. She could smile at shy children or give them a pat or a hug. She could sit with anyone who looked lonely or help a timid child play a game. Even without words there were ways to tell campers, "You are precious. Jesus and I love you." And that is what Naomi tried to do.

But on that hill in back of the tabernacle, Naomi also made a promise to God. She promised, "Some day I will come back to Colombia as a missionary."

Those two weeks seemed to be the shortest weeks in Naomi's life. Suddenly camp was over. It was time to leave—time to fly back to the States. Naomi wrote in her diary, *I can't believe it is all over. . . . I want to go to Colombia and give every last ounce of strength sharing the gospel with these precious people. They need Christ so badly, and they are open to the gospel. They need someone to tell them. I'm willing, and with God's strength I can.*

Then Naomi said goodbye to the campers and the missionaries and flew home to finish college. But after college she did not go back to Colombia. Instead she married a young minister and went to serve Christ with him in an American church. Several years passed. God gave Naomi and her husband two sons, and their work in the American church continued.

What about Naomi's promise to share the gospel with the Colombians? Had she forgotten it? Didn't she want to keep it?

Suddenly one day Naomi had to think about keeping her promise. She had traveled to a missionary conference. All at once, during the conference, memories of Camp Ebenezer and her promise flashed through her mind. Naomi's heart beat fast. Then God spoke to her in words from Ecclesiastes 5:4-5. He said, "When you make a vow to God, do not delay in fulfilling it . . . Fulfill your vow. It is better not to vow than to make a vow and not fulfill it."

God was saying, "When you make a promise, do not put off keeping it, . . . keep your promise. It is better not to make a promise than to make a promise and not keep it." Naomi bowed her head. She knew that she would have to keep her promise.

The Lord not only reminded Naomi to keep her promise—He gave her husband and sons the wish to serve Him in Colombia. How Naomi praised and thanked the Lord!

With glad hearts, Naomi and her family packed up to move to South America—12 years after Naomi made her promise. And instead of one person there were four people to keep the promise—Naomi, her husband and two sons.

How delighted Naomi was to be back in Colombia! And what a surprise the Lord had for her and her family. The first workers' conference they attended was held at Camp Ebenezer. There stood the same tabernacle and in back of it the hill on which Naomi had made her promise to God.

Now Naomi and her family are keeping her promise. How? They are living in the large city of Bogota. They are helping start a church in the part of the city in which they live. They are learning to speak Spanish and are eager to share the gospel with all their Colombian neighbors. But Naomi and her family know that they cannot start a church themselves. It is the Lord God who will help them to keep Naomi's promise and do the work He has given them to do.

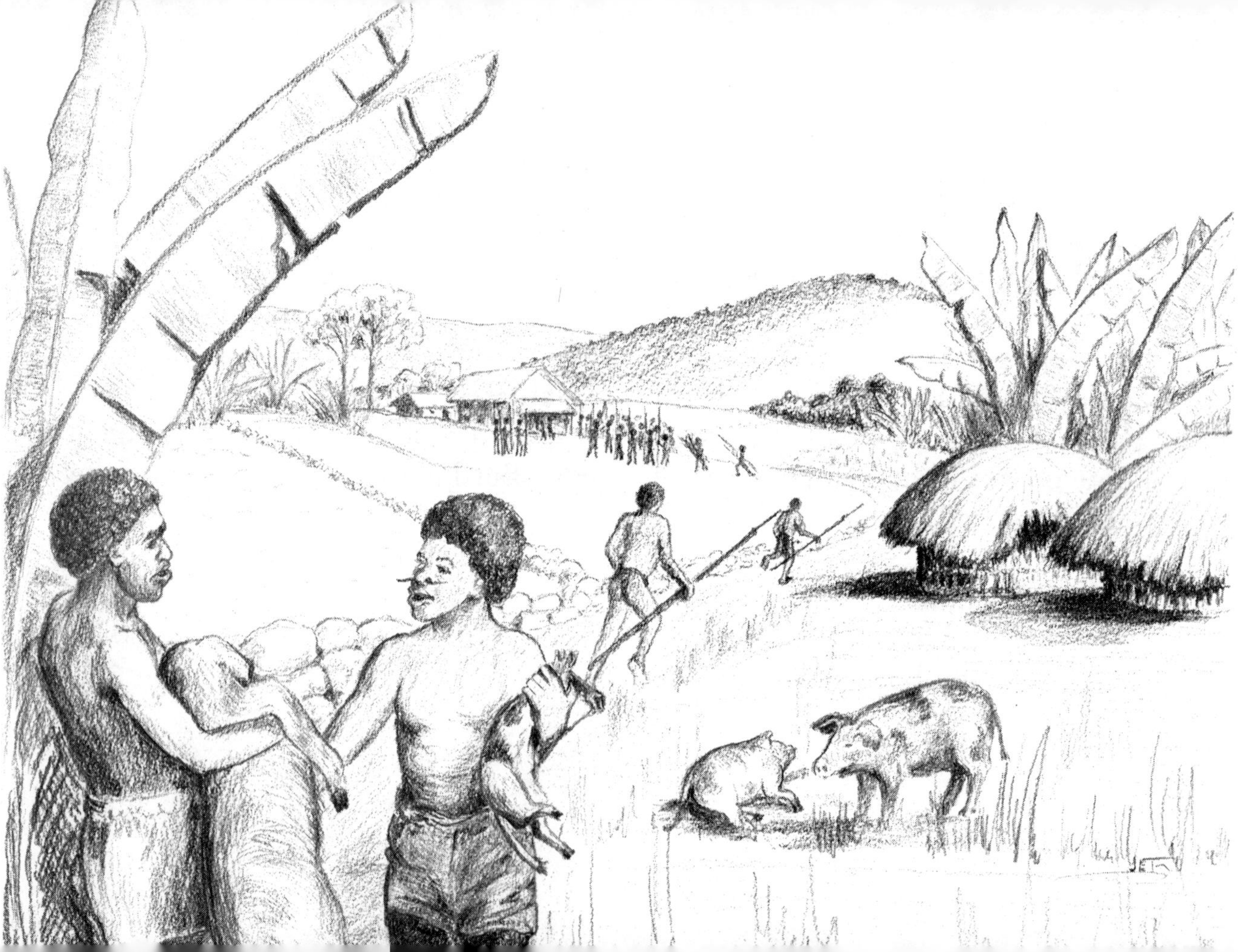

Kill the Missionaries!

It was evening. Some men of the Dani tribe sat around a fire looking worried. They were worried because their pigs were getting sick and dying. Pigs are important to the Danis. They needed pigs to kill for the spirits. All the Danis were afraid of spirits. They said, "If the spirits are not happy, our sweet potatoes will not grow, people will get sick, everything will go wrong."

"The spirits are happy when you kill pigs for them," promised the witch doctor.

"But how can we do that if our pigs get sick and die?" worried the men.

So some men went up the river to see the witch doctor who knew how to make sick pigs well.

"Why," they asked, "are our pigs getting sick?"

"Your pigs are getting sick because the missionaries came to Baliem Valley," said the witch doctor. "The missionaries' skin is different, and their hair is different. They talk about the Creator God and His Son, Jesus. They say He is more powerful than the spirits. The spirits are angry. They are making your pigs sick.

You will have to kill the new missionary people. Then the pigs will get well again."

News of the witch doctor's advice spread to all the villages.

"Kill the missionaries?" asked one man. "Why don't we just chase them out of the valley? They can go back to wherever they came from."

Then a large group of Dani men went to see the missionaries. They announced, "Because of you the spirits are angry and are making our pigs sick. We want you to leave here and go away."

"No," answered the missionaries, "we cannot leave you."

The unhappy men were surprised at the missionaries' answer. They turned and walked home to think about what they should do next.

After that day no one went near the missionaries' house—not even sick people for medicine. Well, there was one boy named Nomalok who still went to their house. Nomalok liked the missionaries. He listened to them tell about the Great God and His Son. Besides, the missionaries, Tuan and Mama, paid him to help them. They paid him for carrying water and firewood.

But suddenly one afternoon two men stepped into the missionaries' yard. They glared at Nomalok and growled, "Get home boy. If you are still here this evening, we will kill you." Then they ran away.

Mama heard the men's threats. She said, "Please go home, Nomalok. You have helped us much. We will pray that God will change people's hearts. And we will pray for the pigs, too. When it is safe you can come again."

Nomalok hurried home. He wondered, *Why don't Tuan and Mama seem afraid, even when men talk about killing them? Is it because they call God their Father?*

At last one day the Dani war chief sent word to all the villages. "The pigs are still getting sick and dying. The witch doctor has said that the missionaries are to blame. Tomorrow we must go and kill them."

Shivers ran up and down Nomalok's back. How could the kind missionaries be to blame for the pig sickness? They helped sick people. Why, when his little sister Walu was dying, the missionaries gave her medicine. They prayed for her to be healed. And she got well. The missionaries had given medicine to many other sick people—and prayed for them, too.

Nomalok was frightened. The warriors planned to kill Tuan and Mama tomorrow. He could do nothing to stop them.

The next day Nomalok watched the warriors begin to gather. Each man carried his long spear, and they met on the hill in back of the missionaries' house.

Missionary Tuan was busy chopping wood. Mama was washing clothes and hanging them on a line. And their children were laughing and playing in the yard.

Don't Tuan and Mama see the warriors? wondered Nomalok. *Aren't they afraid?*

Yes, Tuan looked toward the hill. He saw the warriors with their spears. What did he do? He just called Mama and the children together. Then they bowed their heads.

Nomalok knew that they were talking to their Creator. After they prayed, Tuan turned and walked up the hill. He walked right up to the warriors.

"We want you to go away," said the war chief, looking fierce.

"I can't leave," answered Tuan. "The Creator told me to come and tell you about Him and His Son who died for you. I haven't told everyone yet. Besides, if I left who would give your sick people medicine? Many people who were sick when I came are now well again."

The men hung their heads. They felt ashamed.

"I will pray to the Creator and ask Him to make your pigs well," said Tuan. "And I will pray that you will not kill me so I can keep teaching you words of eternal life and care for your sicknesses."

Then Tuan bowed his head. He prayed for God to protect him and for the sick pigs to get well.

The warriors stood silent and still. They did not know what to say or do. At last Nomalok's father stepped forward. He said, "Tuan is right. Remember how sick my little daughter was? I took her to Tuan and now she is well. Wouldn't it be foolish to kill these missionary friends?"

Nomalok's father pulled his spear out of the ground and walked away. Quietly the other men turned and walked away, too.

That very day the pigs began to get well. And soon the Dani people began to come back to the missionaries' house.

They came for medicine and help. But best of all, they gathered under the trees to listen to the missionaries tell them over and over again about the Creator. Tuan explained how the Creator sent His Son to die for the sins of all kinds of people—those whose skin is black and those whose skin is white.

And one evening Nomalok came to Tuan and whispered, "I want Jesus to wash away my sin. I want to be a child of God." Nomalok was the first Dani to trust in God's Son as his Savior.

Now Nomalok is grown up. He is helping tell his people about the Creator and His Son, Jesus. And far back on the south side of the mountains is a new church of Danis—Danis who trust in the Savior instead of being afraid of spirits.

How glad the Danis are that they did not kill the missionaries!

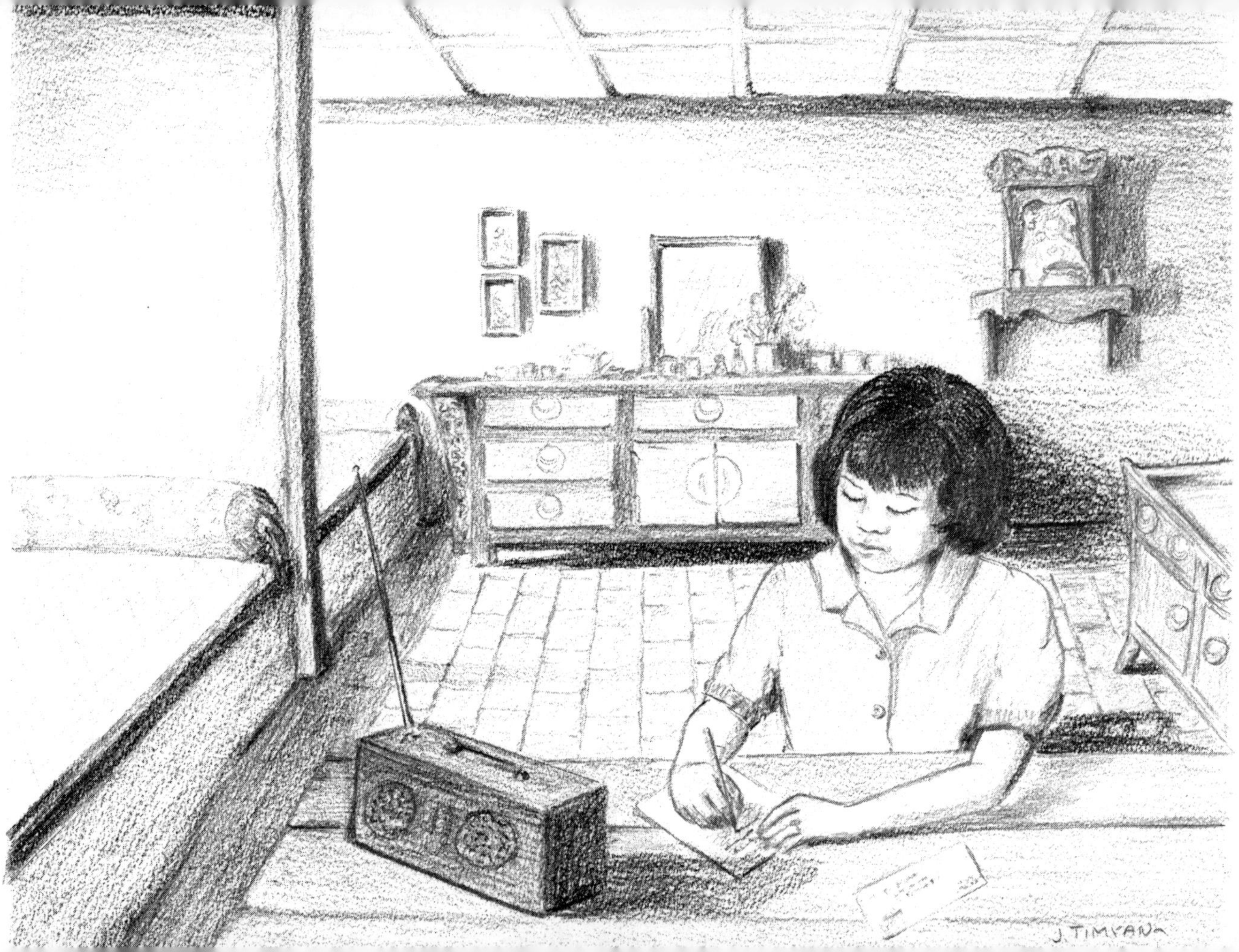
J. TIMYAN

She Heard It on the Radio

How do you feel when someone makes fun of you? Imagine how you might feel if your teacher and classmates laughed at you.

This is what happened to a girl in China one day. Let me tell you why they made fun of her and what she did.

I do not know the girl's name. It could have been something like Lai Chun which means *beautiful pearl*. Lai Chun lives in the large faraway country called the Republic of China.

Even before she began first grade, she went to a school for little children—a kind of nursery school. She began to learn math, the Chinese alphabet and music. And she learned that there is no God to worship or love. Children should honor the great Chinese people and their leaders.

After nursery school and kindergarten, Lai Chun marched off to first grade and then into the grades that followed. She studied her lessons and did all her homework. She and her friends know it is important to study hard, obey their teachers and learn all they can.

But in all of Lai Chun's studies, she

never heard of Sunday school or church. She never saw a Bible or heard about Jesus. But her family had a radio. And one day when she was turning the dial on it, she tuned in to a Hong Kong station—a missionary station. The man on the radio was talking about China.

"What a beautiful country China is. It has great mountains, rivers and plains." Lai Chun nodded. *China is a large, wonderful land. We are an important country*, she thought.

"Do you ever wonder who made your beautiful country?" asked the radio teacher. "Who formed the mountains, rivers and plains? Who put the sun, moon and stars in the endless sky? Where did all the lovely trees, flowers and plants come from?"

Sometimes I do wonder about the world, thought Lai Chun.

"There is a living God—a mighty God—who created China and the world," said the radio teacher. "He is the all-powerful God of heaven and earth. He planned and created everything. If you want to know more about Him, write to this radio station. We will send booklets to tell you about Him."

Lai Chun sat still and wondered, *Is there a God after all? Could there be a God so wise and great that He could make the world?*

She decided, "I will listen to the radio

teacher again another day." And she did. What she heard about God was so new and strange.

"I do not understand about God," said Lai Chun to herself. "Is my schoolteacher right—there is no God? Or is the radio teacher right—there is a living God? I think there might be a great Creator-God. But how can I be sure? I'll write to the radio teacher and ask him to send me booklets about God."

Lai Chun sat down. Carefully she wrote the radio teacher, "I did not believe in God. But after listening to the radio I began to wonder, 'What is God? What will He do to us?' Can you please tell me more about Him and send the booklets."

How happy the radio missionaries were to read Lai Chun's letter! Gladly they mailed her the little booklets about God.

Lai Chun read the booklets and thought about what they said. Every week she listened to the radio teacher, and she began to believe in God who made the world.

But then she had a problem at school. The teacher gave an exam. And one of the questions was, "Is it true that God created man? Write about this question."

I know the right answer to that question, thought Lai Chun. *I can write about that. Yesterday the radio teacher explained that God created the first people.*

On her paper she wrote, "Yes, it is true that God created the first man—and woman. He named them Adam and Eve and. . . ."

Lai Chun was pleased that she knew the right answer to the exam question. But how would her teacher feel about it? Would he be pleased?

A few days later the teacher returned the exam papers and . . . Lai Chun shivered. The teacher looked angry. He handed back all the papers except Lai Chun's. Then he held up Lai Chun's paper before the class and glared at her.

"How can you say there is a God—a God who created people? Did you ever see God? Where did you ever get such an idea?" The children looked at each other and laughed at Lai Chun.

"No god ever made anything," growled the teacher. "Millions and millions of years ago the world just began. It evolved. There began to be some plants and animals. Finally, some animals turned into people. No god could make all that happen," mocked the teacher.

Lai Chun's face turned red. She hung her head. But in her heart she still believed in God. How could such a beautiful world just happen all by itself? Other things like tables, chairs, clocks and pictures don't just happen. Someone thinks about them and makes them.

Lai Chun kept listening to the radio

teacher's lessons about God—and about God's Son, Jesus. But she did not always understand what he said. Again she wrote and asked, "Why are there so many people who do not believe in God? Why can't we see God? How far away is God from us? Does God's Son Jesus live on earth?"

The missionary answered Lai Chun's questions. And he and the other missionaries prayed that God's Spirit would help her understand.

God answered the missionaries' prayers. Lai Chun began to understand about God and His Son. Her heart was filled with wonder that God's Son came to earth and died for her sins. At last she believed in Him. She knew Jesus was her Savior. Happily she wrote to the radio teacher and said, "I am trusting in the Lord Jesus. . . ."

How thankful the missionaries are that Lai Chun belongs to God's family! And it happened because she heard about Him on the radio.

But Lai Chun is not the only listener who has written to these missionaries. Guess how many others from China have written to them. More than 15,000 children, young people and grown-ups! Some of them have believed in the Lord Jesus, too.